HOLOCAUST

The Story of a Survivor

Dee Phillips

SADDLEBACK
EDUCATIONAL PUBLISHING

Yesterday's Voices

Images are in the public domain or courtesy of Shutterstock.

Acknowledgements: With thanks to Lorraine Petersen, Chief Executive of NASEN, for her help in the development and creation of these books.

SADDLEBACK
EDUCATIONAL PUBLISHING
www.sdlback.com

ISBN-13: 978-1-62250-874-7
ISBN-10: 1-62250-874-2
eBook: 978-1-63078-009-8

Printed in Malaysia

20 19 18 17 16   3 4 5 6 7

They took my clothes.
They shaved my head.
I was given a prisoner number.
I was no longer a human.

HOLOCAUST
The Story of a Survivor

In 1939, Germany was at war with
Britain and many other countries.
Germany's leader was Adolf Hitler.
Hitler led a group called Nazis.

The Nazis hated Jewish people.
They bullied Jews.
They made their lives hell.

The Nazis sent Jewish people
to concentration camps.

Six million Jews were killed
in these camps.

This time is known as

THE HOLOCAUST.

Tonight there is a full moon.
I look up and think of Jacob.

I met Jacob in 1939.
He came to teach my
little brother, David.

I would take Jacob coffee.
He would smile at me.
I would smile back.

One evening we went for a walk.
There was a beautiful full moon.
We were so happy.

But life was changing in Poland.

At night my father's friends came.
I would take them coffee.
They talked about the war.
They talked about Hitler
and the Nazis.
They talked about camps
where Jews were slaves.

They said, "It's a bad time to be a Jew."

One day Jacob and I were
in the town square.
A boy spat at Jacob.

The boy said,

"DIRTY JEWS."

I was afraid.

Then the Germans invaded Poland.
Now the Nazis were in charge.
Nazi soldiers came for us.
BANG! BANG! On the door.

"ALL JEWS OUTSIDE NOW!"

We walked to the town square.
I held my little brother's hand.

I saw Jacob.
I said, "I'm afraid.
What if we are split up?"

Jacob said, "I will find you, Sarah.
When there is a full moon,
think of me. I will be
thinking of you."

A soldier shouted at me, "Go left."
To my mother and brother, "Go left."
To my father and Jacob, "Go right."

Jacob shouted, "I will find you!"

David 1939

Mother and Father 1934

The soldiers put us on a train.
The train took us to a camp.

A soldier shouted at me, "Go left."
To my mother and brother, "Go right."
I tried to go right too.
But the soldiers stopped me.

I shouted, "I will find you!"

Tonight there is a full moon.
I look up and think of my family.
I think of Jacob.

It has been 70 years.
But I will never forget.

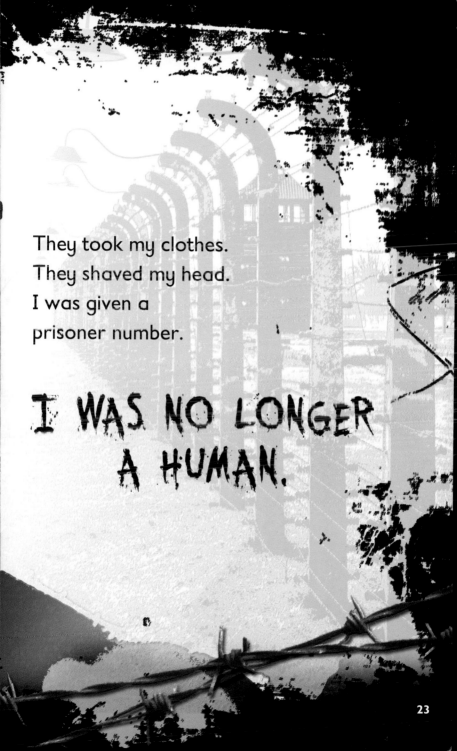

They took my clothes.
They shaved my head.
I was given a
prisoner number.

I WAS NO LONGER
A HUMAN.

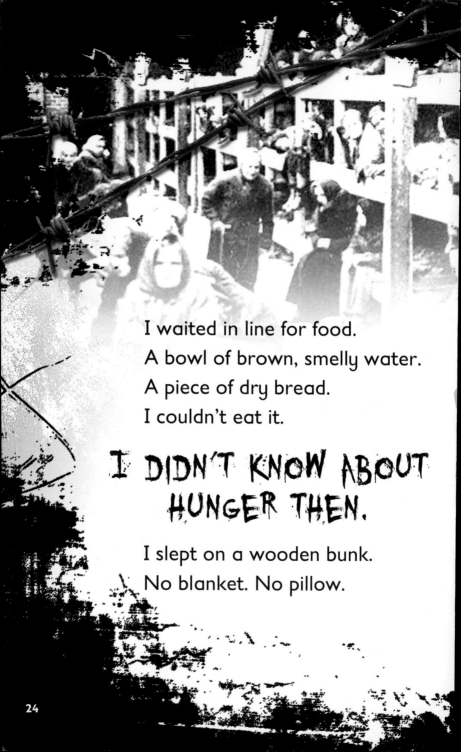

I waited in line for food.
A bowl of brown, smelly water.
A piece of dry bread.
I couldn't eat it.

I DIDN'T KNOW ABOUT HUNGER THEN.

I slept on a wooden bunk.
No blanket. No pillow.

Each morning they counted us.

WE STOOD IN THE ICY RAIN.

IN THE COLD SNOW.

IN THE HOT SUN.

Some women could not go on.

Each day we went to work.
Digging the frozen ground.
Carrying rocks.

I waited for each full moon.
I would think of Jacob.

"I will find you."

I had to keep going.

Weeks and months passed by.
Then years.

We were starving.
My body turned to bones.

MANY WOMEN DIED.

Their bodies were burned.
Women just like me …
                    turned to smoke.

FEGELY MEDIA CENTER

I became ill.
I lay on my bunk.
The guards would shoot me now.

I saw a full moon rising. I said,

"I'm sorry, Jacob,
but I can't go on."

I was ready to die.

I will never forget that next morning.
The guards didn't come.
The American soldiers came.

They told us, "The war is over.
You are free."

I had survived.

The Americans took us to another camp.
There was food and medicine.
There were thousands of men and
women just like me.

I had to find my family.
I had to find Jacob.

David 1939

Mother and Father 193

Every day I looked at lists of names.
I wrote letters.
But I never found my family.
They were all killed.
Killed in the camps.
Killed in the gas chambers.

I kept looking for Jacob.
Was he looking for me?

Tonight there is a full moon.
I look up at the moon.
It has been 70 years.
But I will never forget.

My husband touches my arm.
He says, "I have been looking
for you. Come inside. It's late."

I smile and say, "My Jacob.
Always looking for me."

HOLOCAUST

Behind the Story

In the 1930s, Germany was led by the Nazis. The Nazis needed someone to blame for Germany's problems. One of the groups they picked on was the Jews. Many Jews were beaten, and their homes and businesses were destroyed.

During the Second World War, the Nazis invaded other countries, such as Poland. In those countries, they also singled out certain groups as their enemies. Many people were sent to concentration camps and forced to work as slaves. Most of these people were Jews.

Some concentration camps were called death camps. In these camps, people were shot or sent to buildings known as gas chambers.

These women were freed from the Bergen-Belsen concentration camp in Germany. They are carrying loaves of bread.

Once people were inside a gas chamber, the Nazis released poisonous gas into the building. Hundreds of people were killed at the same time. By the end of the war, millions of people had been murdered by the Nazis.

After the Holocaust

When the war ended, soldiers from America, Britain, and other countries freed the people held in concentration camps.

New camps were set up where survivors could live while they recovered.

Jewish groups tried to reunite families. They made lists of the names of survivors and where those people were living. The lists were then sent to all the different camps.

HOLOCAUST

What's next?

When they are apart, Sarah and Jacob watch for a full moon as a way to stay connected.

Imagine you are about to be separated from someone you love. You cannot text, phone, or contact that person online. Think of some ways to stay connected.

- Wear friendship bracelets.
- Watch our favorite TV show at the same time each week.

Look at how the colors black, gray, and blue are used in the book to show the horror of Sarah's time in the concentration camp.

Think of a time when you felt great pain, sadness, fear, or happiness. Then take a photograph of your face. Using face paint or a computer program, add colors or patterns to your face that show your feelings during that time.

The sadness I felt when Grandpa died.

Sarah and Jacob are characters in a story. Their story, however, is based on what happened to millions of real people because of racism and prejudice. Discuss with your group how the story and the facts you've learned about the Holocaust make you feel. Think about:

• How does it feel to be hated because of your race?

• What did it feel like to be the only person in a family to survive the Holocaust?

Imagine that after the war, Sarah is living at a camp for survivors. One day, a young man arrives at the camp. It is Jacob! He has been searching for her.

With a partner, role-play the couple's meeting.

• What would they say?

• How would they feel?

• How would they have changed?

45

Titles in the

Yesterday's Voices

series

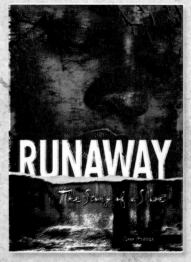

I waited deep below the arena. Then it was my turn to fight. Kill or be killed!

I cannot live as a slave any longer. Tonight I will escape and never go back.

TITANIC
The Story of a Disaster

Dee Phillips

OVER THE TOP
The Story of a Soldier

Dee Phillips

The ship is sinking into the icy sea. I don't want to die. Someone help us!

I'm waiting in the trench. I am so afraid. Tomorrow we go over the top.

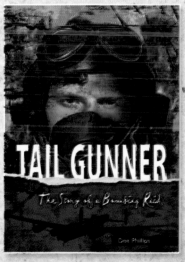

TAIL GUNNER
The Story of a Bombing Raid

Dee Phillips

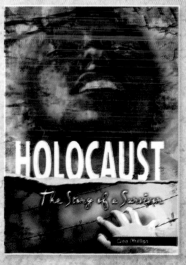

HOLOCAUST
The Story of a Survivor

Dee Phillips

Another night. Another bombing raid. Will this night be the one when we don't make it back?

They took my clothes and shaved my head. I was no longer a human.